Little Eddie

By the Same Author

Published by William Morrow & Company

Published by Harcourt, Brace & World

Little Eddie

WRITTEN AND ILLUSTRATED BY

Carolyn Haywood

WILLIAM MORROW AND COMPANY

NEW YORK, 1947

CONTENTS

Little Eddie

CHAPTER I

WHAT EDDIE BROUGHT HOME

LITTLE EDDIE was the youngest of the four Wilson boys. There was Rudy, aged twelve, the twins, Joe and Frank, who were nine, and Eddie. Eddie was seven.

There were a number of boys and girls in the neighborhood with whom the older boys played, but there were none the same age as Eddie. The older boys were always telling him that he was too little to be in their gang, but this never discouraged Eddie. He just hung around and found ways to get in on nearly everything the older boys did. But sometimes he had to think fast and work hard to do it.

Of all of the girls in the neighborhood, he liked Betsy best. If the boys went off without him, he could go over to Betsy's. Betsy was always glad to see him. Usually, they played checkers.

Little Eddie was very fond of animals. He brought all of the stray animals home with him. Stray cats, stray dogs, birds that had fallen out of their nests, turtles, snails, garter snakes; anything that was alive, Eddie brought home with him. He was always getting fish heads from the fish market for the cats, saving bones for dogs, catching flies for turtles, and putting snails and garter snakes in boxes. His mother complained that every stray cat for miles around could smell the fish heads, and that they all made tracks for the Wilsons' back door; that every dog in the neighborhood knew Eddie's address and that he was always good for a bone. His father said if Eddie brought home another turtle, he would make soup out of it. But none of this discouraged Eddie. He didn't think that the complaining done by his mother and father meant anything.

Eddie had another deep interest. It was in all kinds of signs. He simply loved signs, and every time he saw one he would make one just like it. His bedroom was filled with signs. When you opened Eddie's door, you read, *Stop, Look and Listen, Silence, Men Working, Slow, Danger, Road Under Construction.*

Eddie also brought home junk of all kinds. Every wastepaper basket was hidden treasure to Eddie; when the housecleaning season came around, Eddie could hardly stay in school, he was so afraid he would miss something that was being put out for the rubbish collection.

One corner of the workshop in the basement was supposed to be Eddie's private corner where he could keep his junk. Of course, Eddie didn't call it junk. He called it his valuable property. He had old radio parts, ear phones, old tubes, and dials. Once he came home with an old phonograph horn almost as big as himself. When Eddie left the house, the family had no idea what he would bring back with him. His mother often said that nothing would surprise her. But the day came when she was more than surprised. It was the day Eddie brought home a telegraph pole.

One day Eddie came home with an old filing case which he had found sitting on top of a trash barrel. His bedroom was his office from then on, and he decided he must have a desk. When his father remarked one evening that he was getting a new desk, Eddie piped up, "Can I have the old one, Papa?"

"Nothing doing!" said Rudy. "I'm the oldest. I'm the one that needs the desk."

"No! No!" cried the twins in one breath.

"We get the desk! Don't we, Daddy?" Frank added.

"It was Grandfather's desk," said Joe.

"And we were named after Grandfather," said Frank.

"I ought to chop it up for firewood," said their father. "There isn't a stick of wood left and I can't find any place to buy any. And it's only February. We'll need wood until April."

"Oh, Daddy!" cried Rudy. "You wouldn't burn up Grandfather's desk, would you?"

"I didn't say I would," said his father. "I said I should."

"But you won't, will you, Pop?" said Eddie.

"No, I won't," replied Father. "But I'll tell you

what I will do. I'll give the desk to whichever one of you boys brings in the most wood."

"Oh, Dad!" said Rudy. "Where are we going to get any wood?"

"I don't know," said Father. "But I have tried, and I can't see any reason why you boys shouldn't try. Is it a bargain?"

"Okay," said Rudy.

"Okay," said the twins.

"Okay," said Eddie.

Several weeks passed, and the twins didn't give the wood a thought. They were too busy playing ice hockey to think of wood, and then, one day, Eddie came home with the telegraph pole. It came about in this way.

One afternoon when Eddie came home from school, he found the men from the telegraph company replacing the telegraph pole that stood at the corner of the street on which Eddie lived. Eddie was thrilled. He sat down on the curb on the opposite side of the street and watched every move that the men made. Once he called out, "Would you like to have me help you?"

The man nearest Eddie looked up. "No, thanks,"

he said. "I think we'll be able to do it all by ourselves. You just stay where you are and rest yourself."

Eddie watched the men handle the ropes and he saw the new pole slide into place. Then he looked at the old pole lying in the street. "I certainly would like to have that pole," thought Eddie. "That pole is certainly super." He watched the men as they got ready to move the old pole. Suddenly Eddie said, "If you don't want that pole, I would like to have it."

The men looked at Eddie in surprise. "Now what do you want with a telegraph pole?" the foreman asked.

"Well, my father could use it," said Eddie. "We've been having a hard time to get wood for our fireplace."

"I'm afraid your father will have to get his wood some place else," said the foreman.

"But my father said if I could get him some wood, he would give me my grandfather's desk," said Eddie.

"He did?" said the foreman. Then he looked at the other men. "How about it, fellows? Does the kid get his grandpop's desk?"

"Sure," said one of the men. "Here, sonny! Help yourself to Grandpop's desk."

"Oh, thanks!" said Eddie. Then he added, "I live right up the street in that white house with the white fence. Could you help me carry it home?"

The men laughed. "Help you carry it home, hey?" said one. "Well, fellas, shall we help the big boy carry the little telegraph pole home?"

The five men picked up the telegraph pole and Eddie put his arm around the center of it. Then they all marched up the street, through Eddie's front gate, and put the pole down in the front yard.

"Now I suppose you want us to help you cut it up," said the foreman.

"Oh, no, that's all right," said Eddie. "My father will cut it up."

When Mrs. Wilson came home, she found Eddie sitting on the telegraph pole. "Look, Mother!" he said. "I got the wood for Papa."

"Eddie! Where did you get that!" exclaimed his mother.

"The telegraph men gave it to me," replied Eddie. "Now I'll get Grandad's desk."

"I guess you will," laughed Mrs. Wilson.

When the other boys came home, they were surprised to see the telegraph pole, and when his father heard of how Eddie came home with the telegraph pole, his glasses fell off, right into his bowl of soup.

The day Grandfather's desk was placed in Eddie's room, Eddie put a sign on his door. It said, *Men Working*.

The family, who were downstairs, could hear Eddie scrambling around his room like a squirrel in the attic. They knew what he was doing. He was arranging his office. Then, after a while, his mother noticed that everything was very quiet in Eddie's room. She went to his door and gently opened it. When she looked in, there was little Eddie, with his head on Grandfather's desk, sound asleep. Standing on the desk, and showing above his head, was a sign which said, *Help Wanted*.

His mother called downstairs to his father. Father came upstairs. He picked up Eddie and laid him gently on his bed. His mother undressed him and tucked him under the covers. Through all of this Eddie slept.

As Mother was leaving the room, she saw another sign. She picked it up and hung it on the bed post at the head of Eddie's bed. It said, *Do Not Disturb*.

CHAPTER II

EDDIE AND HIS CATS

ONE day Eddie stopped at the fish market on his way home from school. When Mr. Henderson, the owner of the fish market, saw Eddie come in the door, he said, "Hello, Eddie! What do you want? Fish heads, I'll bet."

"Yepper!" replied Eddie. "You should see the swell cat I have now. She's the biggest cat you ever saw. And a tortoise shell."

"Where do you keep all of the cats you bring home with you?" asked Mr. Henderson.

"Oh, I have a nice little pen for them," said Eddie. "My mother won't let me keep them in the house."

"I should think not," said Mr. Henderson. "Don't the cats ever fight?"

"No," replied Eddie, "they never fight."

Mr. Henderson wrapped some fish heads in a newspaper and Eddie started for home. He hadn't gone far when he came upon a cat. The cat came near Eddie and sniffed. One sniff was enough. The cat ran right along with Eddie. About a block away from his home, Eddie looked down and there was another cat scurrying along beside him.

"Good thing Mr. Henderson gave me a lot of fish heads," Eddie said to himself.

At his own front gate Eddie found still another cat. It joined right up with the others. As they followed Eddie around to the back of the house, Eddie thought, "I never had four cats before. This is wonderful!" But he also thought that he had better not say anything about them to the family.

Eddie put the three cats into the pen with the big tortoise shell cat. He emptied the paper of fish heads into the pen and the cats fell upon them.

"Eddie," his mother called out, as Eddie passed her on the stairs, "you smell of fish. Go and wash your hands. I am going to get rid of that cat, and I don't want you to bring any more cats home with you."

"They don't hurt anything, Mamma, and I keep them in the pen," said Eddie.

"Well, they keep you smelling of fish," said his mother. "And it's awful!"

Eddie went off to wash his hands.

In the middle of the night Eddie was awakened by a horrible noise. He knew at once what it was. The cats were screeching and wailing. He heard his father's footsteps in the hall. Then he heard a window open. Then a splash. He knew that his father had thrown a basin of water out of the window on the cats. "Meow!" said a cat, and then all was silent. A few minutes later, Eddie fell asleep, feeling very sorry for his cats.

The following morning when Eddie appeared at breakfast, his father said, "Now see here, Eddie, I want you to get rid of those cats. And I want you to get rid of them today. Do you understand?"

"But can't I keep the tortoise shell?" asked Eddie.

"You may not keep the tortoise shell, or any other cat," said Mr. Wilson. "We are through with cats."

"Yes, sir," replied Eddie, looking very unhappy.

"What shall I do with them?" Eddie asked.

"I don't know," replied his father. "You brought them here, so you will have to get rid of them."

It was Saturday, so Eddie had the day to get rid of the cats. He found a large wooden box in the garage and put the four cats into the box. Then he put the box in his express wagon and started off. He had no idea what he would do with the cats. He trundled his express wagon along for several blocks until he met a little boy about his own age.

"Would you like to have a cat?" Eddie asked.

"Sure," replied the boy.

"Well, I'll give you one," said Eddie. "They're in my wagon. Which one do you want?"

The little boy looked them over carefully and then he said, "I would like the black-and-white one."

"Okay!" said Eddie, as he picked up the black-and-white cat and handed it to the boy.

"Thanks!" said the boy. "What's its name?"

"I dunno," said Eddie, smoothing the cat's back. Eddie looked at the cat most lovingly. Then he said, "Patches would be a good name. 'Cause it's black-and-white, and it looks just like patches."

"Say, it does, doesn't it?" said the boy. "I guess I'll call it Patches."

Eddie trundled off with his wagon and the three remaining cats. He hadn't gone far when he came upon a man who was repairing his front step. Eddie stopped in front of the man. "Would you like to have a nice cat?" asked Eddie.

"Don't want any cats," said the man.

"My father won't let me keep them," said Eddie in a very sorrowful voice. "And they are awfully nice cats."

"Don't want any, thank you," said the man.

"My father won't let me give them anything to eat," said Eddie.

"Don't want any," said the man.

"And last night my father threw water on them," said Eddie.

"Don't want any," said the man.

"But it would only be one," said Eddie.

"Don't want any," said the man.

"It doesn't cost much to feed one cat," said Eddie. "It doesn't cost anything if you get fish heads from the fish market."

"Don't want any," said the man.

"Oh, dear!" said Eddie. "How would you feel if you were a nice cat and nobody wanted you?"

"Okay!" said the man. "You win, brother. Put the cat down and get out of here."

"Which one do you want?" asked Eddie.

"I don't care," replied the man, without looking up. "Cats are cats. They're all alike to me."

Eddie lifted the big tortoise shell cat out of the box and set her down beside the man. "She's the prettiest cat I ever saw," said Eddie. "And the biggest too. I think you'll like her."

The man grunted, and Eddie and his wagon rattled off with the two remaining cats.

At the next corner he met Billy Porter. "Hi! Bill!" Eddie shouted. "Want a nice cat?"

Billy looked into the box. "What's the matter with them?" he asked.

"Nothing is the matter with them," replied Eddie.

"Well then, why are you giving them away?" asked Billy.

"Pop won't let me keep them," said Eddie.

"Why not?" said Billy.

"Oh, he doesn't 'preciate cats," replied Eddie, picking up the two cats. "Which one do you want?"

"Don't want any," said Billy. "My father doesn't 'preciate cats either."

"Ah, gee!" said Eddie. "Couldn't you just take one?"

"Well," said Billy, "I'll see. Give me the gray one with the white paws. He's pretty."

Eddie handed over the gray cat with the white paws. "You won't be sorry," said Eddie. "He's a nice cat."

"Well," said Billy, "I don't know whether my father will let me keep him."

"So long!" said Eddie, as he rattled away with the one remaining cat.

At the next corner Eddie met Kenny Roberts. "Hey, Ken!" Eddie called out. "Would you like to have a nice cat?"

"No, thanks," said Kenny. "We already have two cats."

"Oh!" said Eddie, and he went on until he reached Betsy's house. There he rang the bell. Lucy, the maid, opened the door. When she saw Eddie she said, "Betsy isn't home, Eddie."

"Oh!" said Eddie. "Well, how would you like to have a nice cat?"

"I wouldn't like it," said Lucy. "We already have a cat and it's one too many, if you're asking me."

"But this is a real nice cat," said Eddie.

"I don't care what kind of a cat it is," said Lucy. "We don't want it."

Eddie turned away, but before Lucy had closed the door he turned back and said, "Maybe some day you'll be sorry you didn't take this cat."

"That's one thing I'm sure I'll never be sorry about," replied Lucy, and she closed the door. Then

she opened it again. "And don't you leave that cat on our front step," she called.

Eddie hadn't thought of leaving the cat on anyone's front step, but now that Lucy had mentioned it, he wondered why he hadn't thought of it before. He trotted right around the block to Mrs. Jackson's house and put the cat on her front porch. While the cat was exploring the porch, Eddie walked away. But he hadn't gotten to the front gate when Clementine, Mrs. Jackson's cook, called out, "Eddie Wilson, you come right back here and get that cat you just put on our front porch. Mrs. Jackson, she don't want any cats 'round here."

"Ah, jeepers!" said Eddie. "Lillybell would like it." Lillybell was Clementine's little girl. "I know Lillybell would like to have a cat."

"No, indeed!" said Clementine. "Lillybell can't have a cat. Those cat hairs go down little Lillybell's throat and give her croup."

"Oh, tarnation!" cried Eddie. "What am I going to do with it?"

"I don't know," said Clementine. "But you can't leave it here."

Eddie went back and picked up the cat. He put it in the box and started off again. About two blocks further on he met Ellen. "Oh, Ellen!" he sang out. "How would you like to have a nice cat?"

"I don't think so," said Ellen.

"Well, just try it over night," said Eddie. "I think you'll like it if you try it."

"Oh, I would like it all right," said Ellen, "but I don't think my family would."

"Just try it," said Eddie. "Just try it over night."

Ellen took the cat. "All right," she said. "But I don't think they will like it."

Now that Eddie no longer had the cats, he ran all of the way home with the express wagon rattling along behind him. He rattled through the front gate and up the front path. Suddenly he stopped. He dropped the handle of the wagon and it fell on the path with a heavy thud. Eddie stood staring at the doorstep. He could hardly believe his eyes, for there sat the great big tortoise shell cat and the black-and-white cat. They were both busy licking themselves.

"Well! I'll be!" exclaimed Eddie. "How did you get here?"

The cats went on, calmly licking.

Just then Eddie looked up the street. He saw Billy Porter coming down the street with a cat in his arms. Before Billy opened his mouth, Eddie knew what was coming. So he was not surprised when Billy called out, "Didn't I tell you? My father doesn't 'preciate cats."

Billy placed the cat back in the box and said, "So long, Eddie. I have to get right back home."

"So long!" said Eddie, in a not very cheerful voice.

While Eddie sat in his wagon looking at the cats, Ellen arrived. "I'm sorry, Eddie," she said, "but my family won't let me keep this cat."

"Not even over night?" wailed Eddie.

"No," replied Ellen. And she placed the cat in the box. "I have to run home," she said. "I have to mind the baby. Good-by."

" 'By!" said Eddie. "I sure think I have a hard life."

And Eddie began to wonder whether he was as fond of cats as he had thought.

CHAPTER III

CATS ARE ALL RIGHT—BUT

EDDIE sat down on his front step and looked at the cats. It had taken him all morning to give them away, and now they were back again. To make things worse, Rudy came home. When he saw Eddie and the cats, he said, "You'd better get rid of those cats before Daddy comes home."

"I know," said Eddie. "I've been trying to get rid of them all morning. They don't stay."

Eddie picked up the big tortoise shell cat and the black-and-white one and put them in the box again. He turned his wagon around and started off. He found the house where the man was repairing his steps.

"Mister," Eddie sang out, "you almost lost your nice cat."

"Is that so?" said the man. "Well, isn't that too bad!"

"But I found her and brought her back to you," said Eddie.

"Is that so?" said the man. "Well, that's too bad."

"Oh, she's a wonderful cat," said Eddie. "You'll be crazy about her."

"Is that so?" said the man. "Well, that will be too bad."

"Mister," said Eddie, "do you mind putting the cat in your house so that she'll kinda know that she belongs to you? She might follow me home."

"Is that so?" said the man. "Well, wouldn't that be just too bad!"

"You bet it would," said Eddie, and he started off with his wagon again.

"Well," thought Eddie, "that's one cat settled, anyway."

He didn't know what to do with the others, so he just trundled them along in his express wagon.

Soon he passed Mr. Stupenfeffer's meat market. The

delivery boy's bicycle was standing outside. Eddie's eye fell upon the wire basket fastened to the handle bars. It contained a small package, but there was still plenty of room for a cat. Eddie knew the delivery boy. His name was Ronny Richards. He was a big boy. He was thirteen years old.

Eddie thought Ronny would probably like to have a cat. He guessed he would put one of the cats in the wire basket. It would be a nice surprise for Ronny. He was sure Ronny would be pleased. He looked over the three cats and decided to give Ronny the gray-and-white one. He was a nice cat.

Eddie lifted the gray-and-white cat out of the box and placed it in the wire basket. He patted it on the head, for he was very fond of the gray-and-white cat. But, although it was hard to part with them, Eddie felt relieved that he now had only two cats left.

He picked up the handle of his wagon, and off he went.

Meanwhile, the gray-and-white cat began to meow. He didn't like being in a wire cage, and his paws didn't feel comfortable. They felt as though they were going through the openings in the basket. In fact, there wasn't anything about the basket that the cat liked. But then he suddenly sniffed something that was very pleasant. It smelled like fresh meat. The cat stopped meowing and sniffed at the package that lay beside him in the basket. Then he scratched the paper. Nothing happened. He decided to try nibbling. So he nibbled and tore a hole in the paper. The odor of meat grew stronger. He nibbled and tore, and nibbled and tore, until he could taste the meat. It was good meat. He had never had such a fine meal. He was in the midst of it when Ronny appeared.

"Say! What's the big idea!" cried Ronny, when he saw the cat. "For Pete's sake! Mr. Stupenfeffer! Look at this cat! It's been eating Mrs. Porter's hamburg steak."

Mr. Stupenfeffer came running out of the store.

"Vell! Take it from the basket, out!" he cried. "The good hamburg steak is ruined already, yet."

Ronny picked up the cat and put it on the pavement, while Mr. Stupenfeffer cried, "You get out of here. Scat mit you!"

The cat flew.

Eddie was still riding the other two cats around the

block. He wished that he could get rid of them both at once.

Suddenly he had a bright idea. He was so pleased with the idea that he began to run. He didn't stop running until he reached the fish market. Then he took the box out of the wagon and carried it in to Mr. Henderson.

"Mr. Henderson!" he cried out. "I got a wonderful idea!"

"You don't say!" said Mr. Henderson. "What is it?"

"Well, you know, when I have the cats at my house," said Eddie, "I have to come over to get fish heads from you, and you have to wrap up the fish heads, and I have to carry them home to the cats. So I figured that it would be much easier if I brought the cats over here, and you could just throw the fish heads to them. That way, they can eat them right here."

"You don't say!" said Mr. Henderson. "And you think that's a swell idea?"

"It's a wonderful idea," said Eddie. "They can eat more here, and maybe you won't have any garbage at all. They're big eaters, Mr. Henderson."

"You don't say!" said Mr. Henderson. "Well, leave

your cats, Eddie, but don't bring any more. Do you understand? I'm not running a cat's restaurant."

"Okay, Mr. Henderson! Okay!" said Eddie. And he scampered out of the door. But he didn't scamper fast enough to miss seeing a gray-and-white cat running towards him. Eddie turned and ran. He ran as fast as he could, but the cat just ran faster. It was no use. There was no escape. The cat had seen Eddie, and Eddie to the gray-and-white cat was an old friend. It kept right after Eddie all the way home.

This would never do. Eddie picked the cat up and carried it to Mr. Henderson's. He opened the door and said, "Mr. Henderson, you wouldn't mind just one more cat, would you?"

"Eddie," cried Mr. Henderson, "you're driving me crazy! Didn't I tell you, 'No more cats'?"

"But, Mr. Henderson," said Eddie, almost in tears.

"Oh, put it down," said Mr. Henderson, "and scram." Eddie put it down and scrammed. He returned home feeling very light-hearted. When he heard his father come in the front door, he ran to meet him. "Say, Pop!" he cried. "You know those cats?"

Eddie's father seemed very much excited. He said,

"Eddie! What did you do with the big tortoise shell cat?"

"I gave it to a man," said Eddie. "And I gave the others to Mr. Henderson, at the fish market."

"Well, Eddie," said his father, "you will have to get that tortoise shell back."

"Why?" asked Eddie.

"Look," said Mr. Wilson. He pointed to the newspaper he was carrying in his hand. "It says here under 'Lost and Found,' 'Lost: Large tortoise shell cat. $25.00 reward.' "

"Jumping grasshoppers!" cried Eddie. "Do you think it's that cat?"

"It sounds like it," said his father.

"Jumping grasshoppers!" cried Eddie, and he ran at top speed down the street.

When he reached the house with the repaired steps, he ran up the steps and rang the door bell. The man to whom Eddie had given the cat opened the door. "You here again?" said the man. "Now what do you want?"

"I came for the cat," said Eddie.

"You came for the cat?" said the man. "What's the

matter with you? Can't you make up your mind?"

"It isn't me," replied Eddie. "It's my father. He changed *his* mind."

"But I like this cat now," said the man. "I think I am going to like her very much."

"Oh, no!" said Eddie. "I don't think you will. She howls something awful sometimes, at night."

"That's just because you don't know how to take care of her," said the man.

"Oh, no!" said Eddie. "She howled, and she howled, and she howled just fierce last night. I think maybe she's sort of a wild cat."

"Here," said the man, picking up the cat. "Take her, and don't let me see this cat again."

Eddie gathered the big cat in his arms and ran all the way home. That night his father drove Eddie and the cat to the address in the paper. Sure enough! It was the lost cat, and the owner gave Eddie the reward of twenty-five dollars. She told Eddie that the cat's name was Prudence, and that she had taken first prize in five cat shows.

"She did!" said Eddie. "I didn't know there were cat shows."

"You didn't?" exclaimed the owner of the cat. "Why! Cat shows are wonderful. I'll give you and your father tickets for the show that is being held next week."

"Oh, that's great!" cried Eddie, but his father just said, "Oh, thank you."

The following week his father took Eddie to the show. Eddie was delighted. He had never seen so many cats or such beautiful cats. He kept saying, "Oh, look, Papa, isn't that a beautiful cat?" And his father would say, "Yes, yes. Very nice."

At last, they came upon a pure white cat, and lying in a basket beside her were three pure white kittens. They were labeled, "Twenty-five dollars each."

"Oh, Papa!" cried Eddie. "Papa! Look at those beautiful white kittens. Oh, Pop!"

"Oh, Eddie!" groaned his father.

"I can have one, can't I, Papa? With my twenty-five dollars. I can, can't I?"

And Papa said, "Oh, Eddie!" as Eddie handed over his twenty-five dollars and carried off a pure white kitten.

CHAPTER IV

UNFAIR TO EDDIE

ONE day as Eddie was walking home from school, he passed a clothing store. Outside of the store, walking up and down, were three men. Each man was carrying a sign which was fastened to the end of a pole. This was a new kind of sign. Eddie stood still and looked at the words on the sign. He could read very well. The first word was "Unfair." Well, he knew what "Unfair" meant. It was what Rudy and the twins were when they wouldn't let him pitch on the baseball team. Only he called it, " 'Tain't fair." Eddie looked at the next word. It was "to." That was easy. First grade stuff. The next word was "Labor." That was a funny word, thought Eddie. He wondered which of the men with the signs was named "Labor."

Eddie stood on the edge of the pavement, watching the men walk back and forth. In a few minutes, along came Mr. Kilpatrick, the policeman. "Run along," he said to Eddie, "you're blocking the sidewalk."

Eddie looked up at the big policeman. "Hello, Mr. Kilpatrick!" he said. "What are they doing?" Eddie rolled his eyes in the direction of the men.

"They're striking," said Mr. Kilpatrick.

"Who?" said Eddie.

The policeman looked puzzled. "I said, they're striking."

"Well, I don't see them hitting anybody," said Eddie.

"They're not hitting anybody," said Mr. Kilpatrick. "It's not that kind of a strike."

"Oh!" said Eddie. "Did they strike out in a baseball game?"

"No!" shouted the policeman. "It ain't got anything to do with baseball."

"Oh!" said Eddie. "Well, what kind of a strike is it?"

"Now, listen to me," said Mr. Kilpatrick, "and I'll make it clear to you. This is a labor strike."

Eddie's bright eyes looked right into Mr. Kilpatrick's. "Uh huh!" he said, and nodded his head. "Which one is Mr. Labor?"

"Nobody is Mr. Labor," said Mr. Kilpatrick. "Labor is the working people."

"Oh!" said Eddie.

"And these working people think the owner of this store is unfair to the people who work for him. Now do you understand?"

"Yes, sir," said Eddie, and his face was as bright as an electric light. "It's just like Rudy and the twins. They're unfair to me."

"Well, I'm glad you got the idea," said Mr. Kilpatrick.

Eddie started off in the direction of home. Mr. Kilpatrick took off his hat and scratched his head. "What a boy!" he said.

As Eddie entered his house, he met his three brothers coming out. Rudy had his baseball bat. Joe had his catcher's mitt, and Frank had his new baseball.

"Can I play?" said Eddie.

"Sure," said Rudy.

"Can I pitch?" asked Eddie.

"Nix!" replied Rudy.

"Catch?" said Eddie.

"Oh, be sensible," said Rudy. "You can't catch."

"First base?" said Eddie.

"Nothing doing," said Joe.

"Second base?" said Eddie.

"No, you don't," said Frank.

"Third base?" said Eddie.

"Say, do you know who we're playing this afternoon?" asked Rudy.

"No. Who?" asked Eddie.

"Why, the Red Foxes. We can't have a little runt like you playing anything important. You can play outfielder or nothing."

"Oh, I always have to play outfielder," said Eddie. "And all I do is run after balls. I won't do it."

"Okay!" said Rudy. "That suits us fine. We don't want you to play anyway." The three boys started for the playground.

Eddie went downstairs to the workshop. There he found a piece of cardboard. He got a jar of paint and a paintbrush, and in bold letters he printed on the card, *Unfair to Eddie.* Then he looked around for a stick, but he couldn't find any. He decided to run over to

Betsy's. Betsy could always find anything that was needed.

When Eddie reached Betsy's house, he found Betsy playing house with her little sister, Star, and Lillybell. When Betsy saw Eddie, she said, "Oh, hello, Eddie! We're playing house. You can be Daddy."

"Nope!" said Eddie. "I'm busy. I'm striking."

"What are you striking at?" asked Betsy.

"I'm striking at the Woodpeckers," said Eddie.

"Now, Eddie!" cried Betsy. "Aren't you ashamed of yourself! You know it's cruel and wrong to hit birds. I won't play with you if you are going to hit woodpeckers."

"Not birds, Betsy! Not birds!" cried Eddie. "The ball team! You know! Rudy's Woodpeckers."

"Oh, them!" said Betsy. "What have they done to you now?"

"They won't let me play anything but outfielder," said Eddie.

"They won't let *me* play at all," said Betsy.

"Well, I'm striking," said Eddie. "Look!" And at this point Eddie held up his sign. "Have you a stick that I can fasten this to?"

"Come out into the garage," said Betsy. "I guess we can find something."

Betsy led the way to the garage, and Eddie and the little girls followed. In the corner of the garage Betsy found a stick about three feet long. "Here, this will do," she said.

"Oh, that's great!" said Eddie.

Betsy watched Eddie fasten the card to the stick with three thumbtacks. "Where are you going with it?" asked Betsy.

"Over to the playground," said Eddie. "The Woodpeckers are playing the Red Foxes. I'm going to walk up and down and strike."

"Boy! Oh, boy!" cried Betsy. "This is going to be super. I'm coming with you."

Eddie's face lit up. "Say, Betsy," he said, "how about you carrying a sign, too?"

"Sure!" said Betsy. "I'll carry a sign." And Betsy dashed into the house for a piece of cardboard.

When she returned, Star said, "Star carry sign." And Lillybell said, "Me carry sign, too."

"Oh, dear!" said Betsy. "There isn't any more cardboard, and I only have one more stick."

Star puckered up her face and began to cry. "Star want to carry sign," she cried.

"Here!" said Eddie, picking up an old umbrella. "You can carry this."

Eddie put the umbrella up. Five bare ribs stuck out, but the rest of the ribs were still covered with black silk. With a piece of white chalk Eddie wrote on the black silk, *Unfair to Eddie.*

"Lillybell want umbrella, too," said Lillybell.

"You and Star can both walk under this one," said Eddie. "See? You can carry it together."

The two little girls were delighted as they set forth with the umbrella. Eddie led the parade, followed by the little ones. Betsy brought up the rear. They walked over to the playground. They could see the boys busy with their game. There were Rudy and the twins, Billy Porter, Richard and Henry, Kenny Roberts, and Christopher. The whole gang was there. They were in the midst of the game with the Red Foxes. The Red Foxes were making a home run when Eddie's parade appeared. All of the Woodpeckers were jumping up and down and shouting: "Get him! Get him out!" "Throw it here!" "Oh, Gee! Don't be so dumb! That was dumb!" Kenny, who was playing outfielder, was chasing the ball while one of the Red Foxes made a nice home run.

When the two teams calmed down, they saw Eddie and his parade. They were walking up and down a near-by path.

"Look at Eddie!" cried Billy Porter. "He's striking at us!"

"Well, it won't do him any good," said Rudy.

"He's too little to play on this team. He can strike all he wants to, but it won't get him on this team."

"Betsy's striking, too," said Kenny.

"Oh, Betsy always takes Eddie's part in everything," said Rudy. "We're not going to have her on the team."

"She was pretty good on the football team," said Kenny.

"Well, this is different," said Rudy. "Come on now, fellas. Our side up to bat. We have to get this one. Score's eight to seven."

"Yah!" cried the Red Foxes, "eight to seven, favor the Red Foxes." All of the Red Foxes yelled long and loud.

Eddie and Betsy, and the little girls with the umbrella, walked up and down during the next inning while the Woodpeckers again lost to the Red Foxes.

"Trouble with the Woodpeckers is they can't run," said Betsy.

"They can't bat, either," said Eddie. "I never saw such batters. Look at Joe swinging like a windmill."

Just then Mr. Kilpatrick appeared. "Hello, Mr. Kilpatrick!" cried Betsy. "Eddie's striking against the Woodpeckers."

"I thought he would be striking against something," said Mr. Kilpatrick. "I could see he liked the idea when I was talking to him this afternoon. How's the game going?"

"Fierce," said Eddie.

"The Woodpeckers are losing," said Betsy.

"Won't they let you play?" asked Mr. Kilpatrick.

"No," replied Eddie, "they say I'm too little. But I can run fast, Mr. Kilpatrick. You should see how fast I can run."

"Do you think you could bat?" asked Mr. Kilpatrick.

"Sure!" said Eddie. "I could bat a home run."

"Well, I wouldn't boast if I were you," said Mr. Kilpatrick. "You had better do it first and boast afterwards."

Just then the inning was over, and again the Red Foxes had scored a run. They were screaming with joy.

Mr. Kilpatrick walked up to Rudy. "Rudy," he asked, "are you captain of the Woodpeckers?"

"Yes, sir," said Rudy.

"Well then, I want you to be fair to Eddie and try him out on your team."

"Now?" wailed Rudy. "When we're losing?"

"Yes, now," said Mr. Kilpatrick.

"Oh, boy! This is going to be good!" cried one of the Red Foxes. "With that little runt on their team, we'll wipe up the diamond with them." And all of the Red Foxes laughed and yelled.

"And I want you to let Betsy have a try at this, too," said Mr. Kilpatrick.

"Betsy!" wailed all of the Woodpeckers in a chorus.

"Yes, Betsy!" said Mr. Kilpatrick. "Some girls play good baseball."

When the Red Foxes heard this, they turned somersaults and stood on their heads. They jumped up and down and yelled, "Oh, fellas, this is going to be apple pie for us."

The Woodpeckers sulked.

Mr. Kilpatrick turned to the roaring Red Foxes. "Now," he said, with a twinkle in his eye, "you fellas will have to take the other two."

"What other two?" said the captain of the Red Foxes.

"Why, these two!" said Mr. Kilpatrick, pointing to Star and Lillybell.

"Mr. Kilpatrick!" shrieked the Red Foxes. "Those babies can't play baseball!"

Now it was the Woodpeckers' turn to stand on their heads and double over laughing. Billy and Christopher tried to help matters along, so they pushed Star and Lillybell towards the Red Foxes. But this was too much for Star and Lillybell. They didn't know what they were being pushed into, but they knew they didn't like it. They both turned and ran to Mr. Kilpatrick, and began scrambling right up the big policeman's legs.

Mr. Kilpatrick laughed and picked one up in each arm. "Well," he said, "I guess they don't want to play baseball. We'll stand over here and watch the game."

In the next inning, Betsy played second base and Eddie played third. The first Red Fox up to bat was put out by Betsy. The second reached first base. The third got to first base, while the boy on first reached third. The next fellow struck out. The Woodpeckers began to feel more hopeful. Then the fourth player came to bat. He got a base on balls. Now all of the bases were full. Eddie's hands were wet with excitement as the next player came up to bat. He watched him swing.

He heard the whack as the bat hit the ball. Then he saw the ball coming straight towards him. He held out his hands, and felt the hardness of the ball. It stung his hands but he didn't drop it.

The Woodpeckers nearly went wild. They roared with joy. The inning was over.

When the Woodpeckers came up to bat, Betsy made a home run with the bases full. At the end of this inning the game was theirs. The Woodpeckers had won, eleven to nine.

The Woodpeckers ran to Mr. Kilpatrick, shouting, "Did you see that, Mr. Kilpatrick? Wasn't that wonderful, Mr. Kilpatrick?"

"Now," said Mr. Kilpatrick, "maybe you'll trust my judgment in the future. Maybe you see that I know a thing or two."

Eddie was so pleased he looked ready to burst, and Betsy's face was shining.

Eddie walked over to where he had left his sign and the umbrella. He picked up the umbrella and rubbed the words off. Then he picked up the signs. He laid them on the ground and got down on his knees. He reached into his pocket and took out a piece of white

chalk. With the chalk, he carefully covered the black letter "u" and the letter "n" on each sign. He handed one to Betsy and took the other himself, and all of the Woodpeckers traipsed home led by Betsy and little Eddie, carrying signs that read *Fair to Eddie.*

CHAPTER V

LITTLE EDDIE GOES TO TOWN

IT was half-past three of a Saturday afternoon when Mrs. Wilson remembered that she needed a jar of cold cream. She looked around the house to see if one of the older boys was at home, but she only found little Eddie. Eddie was busy oiling an old typewriter that he had picked up in a junk shop for a dollar. It was his most recent treasure. About half of the keys were gone, and the rest made a noise like a string of freight cars going over a bridge. Eddie thought a little oil would help. He was busy pumping sewing machine oil into every crack in the typewriter when his mother found him.

For a few minutes she stood watching him. He looked very little. She wondered whether to send him for the cold cream. He had never been to the center of the city alone. He would have to change buses, and Mrs. Wilson wondered whether Eddie was big enough to change buses. At last she said, "Eddie, do you think you could go to the city for Mother? I need a jar of

cold cream from Potter's Drug Store. Mr. Potter makes his own cold cream, and I like it much better than any other."

Eddie looked up with his eyes sparkling. "Oh, Mamma!" he cried. "Sure, I can go to the city."

"You know, you have to change buses," she said. "You have to change to the 'H' bus."

"Sure! I know," said Eddie, wiping his hands on his trousers.

"Eddie!" cried Mrs. Wilson. "How often do I have to tell you not to wipe your hands on your trousers?"

"I'm sorry," said Eddie. "I forgot."

"Well now, don't forget that you are going to get cold cream. And remember that you change to the H bus and get off at Twelfth Street."

"I know. I know," said Eddie. "And Potter's Drug Store is right on the corner."

"That's right," said his mother. "I'll write a note for you, and you can give it to Mr. Potter."

"Oh, that's the way babies go to the store," said Eddie. "I'm no baby. I'm not going to hand Mr. Potter a piece of paper. I can remember cold cream."

"Well, run along and get washed, and put on a clean shirt and your other trousers," said his mother.

Eddie went off to wash. In about ten minutes he was ready.

"I'll put you on the bus," said Mrs. Wilson, handing Eddie his bus fare. "And I'll ask the bus driver to put you off to change to the H bus."

"Oh, Mamma," said Eddie, "let me tell him. He'll think I'm a baby if you tell him. When I get in I'll say, 'I want to change to the H bus.'"

"No, Eddie," said his mother, "you must say, 'Will you please tell me where I get off to take the H bus.' Then sit close to the driver."

"Okay," said Eddie.

"And don't lose your yellow transfer that the bus driver will give you. That's your fare on the H bus."

"Okay," said Eddie.

"And ask Mr. Potter to show you where you get the bus to come home. Don't forget you have to change to the E bus to come home."

"I know," said Eddie. "I know."

"And don't forget what it is you are going for," said Mrs. Wilson. "Cold cream."

"I won't forget," said Eddie. "Rudy says if you want to remember something, you think of something that goes with it. You know. If you want to remember eggs, you think of chickens. I'll keep thinking of milk, and then I'll remember cold cream."

"You just keep thinking of cold cream," said his

mother. "And tell Mr. Potter to charge it on my bill."

"But I want to do it Rudy's way. I want to think about milk," said Eddie.

"Here comes the bus," said his mother.

The bus swung up to the curb, and before the door opened Eddie said, "You won't tell the bus driver, will you, Mamma? I want to tell him."

The door opened, and Eddie stepped into the bus. He handed his fare to the driver and said, "I'm going to the city for my mother. I have to change to the H bus. I think I know where to get off, but I guess you had better tell me." Then he added, "Please."

"All right," said the driver. "Here's your transfer. Hold on to it. And sit right there."

Eddie sat down in the seat the driver pointed out. Beside Eddie sat a very fat man, so there wasn't much room for Eddie. He wriggled back on the seat, and his legs dangled over the edge.

In the seat behind Eddie sat a woman with a baby on her lap. On the seat beside her lay a large green watermelon.

The bus rolled rapidly along, and Eddie bounced a little on his seat and swayed from side to side. The straw-covered seat was very slippery, and the fat man took up the greater part of the seat.

Suddenly the bus gave a terrible lurch as it swung around the corner. All of the passengers swayed with the bus. The watermelon on the seat behind Eddie rolled off the seat. The lurch of the bus threw it forward, and it landed with a smack in the aisle of the bus. A split second later Eddie shot off his seat and "Kerplunk!" he sat right on the watermelon. The fall to the floor had already cracked the watermelon, so when Eddie sat on it, it smashed into pieces, splashing in all directions.

The bus driver drew up to the curb and stopped. "Anybody hurt?" he called out, as he turned in his seat.

Everyone in the bus was standing up. The fat man was leaning over Eddie. "Are you hurt, son? Are you hurt?" he was saying to Eddie. Eddie was lying flat on the floor now, surrounded by pieces of watermelon. He didn't look exactly scared, but he looked terribly surprised. The man held out his hands to him and Eddie took hold of them. "There's something the matter with the seat of my trousers," he said.

"Well, stand up," said the bus driver, who had left his wheel. "Let's have a look."

Eddie got up and turned his back on the driver. Then he leaned over. The whole seat of his trousers was wet.

"Does it hurt?" said the bus driver.

"Is it blood?" asked Eddie, hoping that it was.

"No," replied the bus driver. "It's watermelon. I said, does it hurt?"

"No," said Eddie. "Just awful wet."

When the lady with the baby found that Eddie was all right, she began to think about her watermelon. "What about my watermelon?" she said to the bus driver. "I paid a dollar for that watermelon."

"I'm sorry, madam," said the bus driver, "but you had no right to have the watermelon on the seat. We charge for those seats, and you didn't pay any fare for the watermelon."

"Well!" said the lady. "We'll just see about this. I'll take it up with the company."

"Very well, madam," said the driver, as he picked up the pieces of watermelon and put them in a newspaper. When he had gathered it all up, he turned to the lady. "Madam," he said, holding out the bundle, "your watermelon."

"Throw it out," said the lady.

As he opened the door of the bus, Eddie said, "Hey! What are you going to do with it?"

"I'm going to throw it down the sewer," said the bus driver.

"Oh, Mister!" Eddie cried. "Wait a minute! Can I have a piece?"

"Sure!" said the bus driver. "Help yourself!"

Eddie selected one of the larger pieces and settled back in his seat, while everyone, even the lady with the baby, laughed.

The fat man on the seat beside him bounced up and down when he laughed. "Here," he said, placing his newspaper on Eddie's lap, "have a napkin."

Eddie hadn't half finished his piece of watermelon when the bus driver called out, "Walnut Street. Change to the H bus. This is it, son."

Eddie scrambled off his seat, knocking the newspaper from his lap. The bus stopped, and Eddie stepped out.

"So long!" the bus driver called to him.

"So long!" Eddie called back. Then, as the door was closing, he held up the piece of watermelon and shouted, "Thanks!"

He finished the watermelon while he waited for the H bus. As it came into sight, he threw the watermelon rind down a near-by sewer. He stepped into the bus, and hoped that no one would notice his trousers. They still felt wet, and they were beginning to feel sticky.

"Fares!" said the bus driver. And then Eddie thought of his transfer ticket for the first time. He looked in both of his hands but it wasn't there. He put his hand in his trouser pocket, and pulled out a handful of odds and ends. A bunch of rusty keys, some bottle tops, a few marbles, a couple of large screws, some nuts and bolts, a small flashlight, a piece of white chalk, some broken crayons, a ball of string, and a quarter. But there was no transfer ticket.

"Sit down," said the bus driver. "I can't wait all day."

Eddie sat down and plunged his hand into his other pocket. He pulled out a handful of cornflakes. He had put them there after breakfast to nibble on. Then he had forgotten them. Now in the excitement of looking for the transfer ticket, the cornflakes fell in a shower to the floor.

At the next stop the bus driver looked around. "How are you coming?" he said to Eddie.

"I've got it some place," said Eddie.

"Try the pocket of your shirt," the driver suggested.

Eddie poked his fingers into his shirt pocket. A wide grin spread over his face, and he pulled out the yellow transfer ticket. "I knew I had it," he said, as he handed it to the driver. Then he added, "Oh, I forgot. We didn't go past Twelfth Street, did we?"

"Two more stops," said the driver.

Eddie ate his few remaining cornflakes, and at the second stop he jumped out the moment the doors opened.

He walked into Potter's Drug Store and up to the counter. Mr. Potter came out from behind a glass window through which Eddie could see shelves filled with bottles. Every time he came into Potter's he wished that he could go behind that window and play with all of those bottles.

"Hello!" said Mr. Potter. "You're Mrs. Wilson's little boy, aren't you?"

"Yes, sir," replied Eddie. "I'm Eddie."

"Well, what can I do for you, Eddie?" Mr. Potter asked.

"Mamma sent me for some . . . some . . . some . . ."

"Yes?" said Mr. Potter. "Some what?"

"Uh, some . . ." What was it his mother had sent him for. Eddie couldn't remember.

"Did she write it down for you?" asked Mr. Potter.

"No," said Eddie. "But I remember what it was."

"You do?" said Mr. Potter.

"Yes. It was, ah . . . It was, ah . . . Milk!"

"Milk!" exclaimed Mr. Potter. "Eddie, I don't think your mother sent you here for milk."

"Well, it wasn't just milk, but it was some kind of milk," said Eddie.

"Oh, I know!" said Mr. Potter. "Milk of magnesia." And with this, Mr. Potter placed a package on the counter.

"I don't think it was milk of magnesia," said Eddie.

"Maybe it was shoe milk," said Mr. Potter. "There's a shoe milk to clean white shoes. Do you think it was shoe milk?" Mr. Potter lifted a package off a shelf and placed it beside the milk of magnesia.

"Shoe milk. Shoe milk," repeated Eddie. "It didn't sound like that."

Mr. Potter's face lighted up. "I know," he said, "it was probably malted milk. Was it malted milk, Eddie?"

"Malted milk," said Eddie. "Malted milk. Well, now, maybe it was." Mr. Potter brought out the bottle of malted milk.

"No," said Eddie, wrinkling up his brow. "I don't think it was malted milk."

Mr. Potter placed his palms on the counter and leaned towards Eddie.

"Eddie," he said, "do you think it was buttermilk soap? Try to think hard. Was it buttermilk soap?"

"Buttermilk soap," muttered Eddie. "Buttermilk soap."

Mr. Potter placed a cake of buttermilk soap beside the other packages.

"Maybe it was," said Eddie, "but I'm not quite sure."

"You're sure it wasn't milkweed lotion?" said Mr. Potter.

"What's that for?" Eddie asked.

"It's for your hands. Keeps them soft," replied Mr. Potter.

"Milkweed, milkweed," Eddie mumbled to himself. "Milkweed."

"Well, one of these must be right," said Mr. Potter. "Tell you what we'll do. I'll put all of these things in a bag and you take them home to your mother. She can bring back the ones she doesn't want."

"Okay!" said Eddie, joyfully. "That's a good idea, Mr. Potter."

Mr. Potter placed all of the packages in a large paper bag. "I'll charge this on your mother's bill," he said. "You tell her she can return what she doesn't want."

Eddie took the bag in his arm. Then he said, "My mother said, 'Will you please show me where to get on the bus to go home?'"

"Why, of course," replied Mr. Potter, coming out from behind the counter. "Come along."

Mr. Potter walked outside with Eddie. "You get the H bus right over on that corner. Now wait until the light changes."

Eddie watched the traffic signal. When it turned green, Mr. Potter said, "Now, go ahead. And remember to change to the E bus at Walnut Street."

Eddie ran across the street with his large package. As he reached the pavement he could see the H bus coming. Just as it swung up to the curb, Eddie thought of milk again. Milk. The door opened and he put one foot on the step. Then he jumped back. He looked at the traffic signal. It was green. He dashed across the street and into the drug store. He ran up to the counter and put down his bundle. Then he shouted, "Cold cream! It was cold cream!"

Mr. Potter came out from behind his window. "So! It was cold cream! Are you sure?"

Eddie nodded his head very vigorously. "Yes, Mr. Potter. I know it was cold cream. Do you want to know how I know?"

"Yes," said Mr. Potter. "How do you know it's cold cream?"

" 'Cause I kept remembering milk," said Eddie.

CHAPTER VI

VOTE FOR ME

E DDIE stood on the corner waiting for the bus.
He looked up the street, but the bus was no-
where in sight. He decided to walk to the next bus
stop. Eddie could see a banner stretched across the
street away up in the center of town. Eddie loved ban-
ners. They always said something exciting. He could
see that it had letters painted on it. He guessed he
would walk up and see just what the letters said. When
he reached the next bus stop, the H bus drew up to

the curb but Eddie didn't notice it. He was too busy straining his eyes to read the words on the banner. He hoped it said that the circus was coming to town. Eddie loved the circus.

He walked another block. Then he stood still on the corner. The letters showed plainly now. There were four words, but his eyes fastened on the last two. To his utter amazement, those two words were his name. "Edward Wilson." His very own name! "Edward Wilson." In great big black letters, away up on

the big banner, stretched across the main street. What was his name doing up there? he wondered. He moved his eyes from his name to read the first two words. They were, "Vote for." Then he read the whole sign. *Vote for Edward Wilson.* The last time he had seen a banner like that it was about voting for the President of the United States. Now it was about voting for Edward Wilson, and he was Edward Wilson. Eddie wondered what he was going to be voted for. Maybe he was going to be President of the United States.

Just then an H bus pulled up at the curb. Eddie stepped in. He handed his fare to the bus driver and remembered to ask for a transfer. He sat down beside a tall thin man. He was just as thin as the man who had ridden into town with Eddie was fat. Eddie thought he looked exactly like the picture of Jack Spratt in his old nursery rhyme book. Eddie wriggled back in his seat until his shoulders rested against the back of the seat. Then he looked up at the man.

"Mister," he said, "am I going to be President of the United States?"

"Well, I wouldn't be surprised!" said the man.

"Are you going to vote for me?" asked Eddie.

"Sure, I'll vote for you," the man replied. "Do you think you will like being President?"

"Oh, sure!" said Eddie. "Of course I'll like being President of the United States. You ride in a parade when you're President, don't you?"

"Oh, my yes!" said the man. "You ride in a big automobile."

"Oh, heck!" said Eddie. "I'm not going to ride in any automobile. I'm going to ride on a white horse, like the pictures of George Washington."

"I see," said the man. "I agree with you. A white horse is much more elegant."

"Do you think they will let me have a white horse when I'm President? You don't think they'll make me ride in an old automobile, do you?" asked Eddie.

"They will have to let you have a white horse," said

the man. "After all, when you're the President, you can have anything you want."

"Oh, boy!" said Eddie, gazing up at the ceiling of the bus with a dreamy look in his eyes. "I'm going to have molasses cocoanut strips every morning for breakfast instead of making believe my bacon is cocoanut strips. And I'm going to have a soda fountain right on the top of my desk, and when I pull out the drawer it will be full of ice cream."

"Walnut Street!" the bus driver called out. "Change for the E bus."

Eddie came out of his day dream with a start. He scrambled down off the seat. "This is where I get off," he said to the man. "So long!"

"So long!" said the man. "Don't forget me when you get into the White House."

"I won't," said Eddie, moving toward the door. Just as he was about to step out, he turned back. "What's your name?" he called.

"Wilson," replied the man.

Eddie was so surprised he nearly fell on his face as he left the bus.

He soon forgot it, however, as he boarded the E bus. He gave the yellow transfer ticket to the bus driver, and found a seat beside a man who was reading the newspaper. Eddie looked at as much of the paper as he could see. He couldn't read anything but there were some pictures. There was a little girl eating a candy bar. There was a picture of a dog sitting up on his hind legs. Eddie knew what that meant. It meant Puppy Biscuits. There was a lady in a fur coat, and a picture of a man tying his necktie. Then Eddie's eye fell upon one corner of the page that he could see and read. There, in large letters with a lot of white space around them, was his name again. He read "Vote for Edward Wilson."

Eddie looked up into the man's face and said, "Mister, are you going to vote for Edward Wilson?"

The man lowered his paper with a great rustling noise. "I should say not!" he boomed out in a great big voice. Eddie was so startled that he nearly fell off his seat again. "Edward Wilson is good for nothing! I wouldn't vote for him for anything! Why Edward Wilson wouldn't make a tenth-rate dog catcher. Bah!"

With this, the man got up and started for the door.

Eddie got down off his seat and followed him. "I don't think you're very polite," said Eddie.

"I don't have to be polite," said the man. "Not about Eddie Wilson."

As the door opened, Eddie said, "That's not true."

"What isn't true?" bellowed the man, as he stepped down.

"I would so make a good dog catcher," cried Eddie, as the door closed on the man.

As Eddie went back to his seat, he wondered why everyone in the bus was laughing. He didn't see anything to laugh about. Well, anyway, he had learned one thing. He wasn't going to be President of the United States. He was going to be the dog catcher. He wouldn't ride a white horse and have a soda fountain on his desk with ice cream in the drawer, but it would be exciting to catch dogs.

Soon Eddie reached his own corner. He stepped out of the bus and ran the rest of the way home. He passed Rudy and the twins, who were playing marbles. "Hi, fellas!" Eddie shouted. "Vote for me!"

He pushed open the front door and met his father in the hall. "Hello, Daddy!" he cried. "I'm going to be the dog catcher. I'm going to be the dog catcher, Daddy."

"Don't shout so, Eddie," said his father. "Don't shout."

Eddie found his mother in the kitchen. "I got the cold cream, Mamma," he said.

"Good for you!" said his mother.

"And I did it Rudy's way. I just kept remembering milk," said Eddie. "I told you that was a good way, didn't I tell you, Mamma?"

"Yes, you did, Eddie," replied his mother. "I think it's wonderful that it worked so well."

"Oh, it's a good way," said Eddie. "Mamma, are you going to vote for me?"

"Yes, indeed, darling," said his mother. "I'll vote for you for anything."

When Eddie appeared at dinner, he had a sign hanging around his neck. It said, *Vote for me.* All through the meal he kept making remarks about being the dog catcher, but no one paid any attention to him. Mother was busy talking about Aunt Bessie's baby; Father talked about a new kind of glue; and Rudy and the twins talked about the Big League baseball teams. No one paid any attention to little Eddie except that every time Eddie said, "Mamma, will you vote for me?" his mother replied, "Of course, darling. I'll vote for you."

The following Friday, Eddie was walking home from school his favorite way. It led past the backs of some stores and offices. Eddie loved this way home from school, and Fridays were always best. Friday was rubbish day, and sometimes there were treasures sitting out waiting for the rubbish men.

Today Eddie's eyes fell upon a wooden box. He looked at it carefully, and his eyes grew large at the thought of the treasure inside. It had a sliding lid which pleased him very much indeed. He pushed it with his finger. The lid was very tight. He sat down on a barrel and worked over the lid for a long time. Finally, he felt it slip a little bit. He pushed and pushed. At last it was off. At first Eddie was deeply disappointed, for it looked as though the box contained nothing but an old newspaper that had been stuffed inside. As he removed the newspaper, he noticed that it was very yellow with age. He looked at the date. He always looked at the date on old newspapers. His father had told him that sometimes **very** old newspapers were valuable. This one was dated November, 1912. Across the top of the paper in very big letters Eddie read, "Wilson elected President of the United States." Eddie knew that it didn't mean that he, Eddie Wilson, had been elected President of the United States. He knew that 1912 was long before he had been born.

Eddie stuck the paper under his arm and lifted a piece of cardboard out of the box. Under the cardboard there were buttons. Buttons with pins on them. He took out a handful and, to his great surprise, on each button was printed "Wilson." Eddie's face shone. This was treasure! Wilson buttons! He pinned a whole row of them on his coat. Then he picked up the box and started for home.

When he reached home, he showed the buttons to his brothers. Of course they wanted buttons right away. Buttons with their name on them were wonderful.

"Hey, where did you get them?" Rudy asked.

"I found 'em," said Eddie.

"Boy! You sure do find nice stuff," said Joe. "Here, give us a handful."

"No," replied Eddie. "I'm going to sell them. A cent apiece."

"Ah, you can't sell those old buttons," said Rudy. "Give us some."

"Well, I'll give you each one," said Eddie, holding out three buttons."

Each of his brothers took a button. "You'll never sell those buttons," said Rudy.

"Yes, I will," said Eddie.

"Eddie's crazy," said Rudy. "Just plain crazy. He's always shouting 'Vote for me.' Who does he think he is?"

CHAPTER VII

EDDIE THE DOG CATCHER

THE following day, Eddie spent the morning in the basement. He was busy making a dog-catcher's net. After all, if he was going to be elected dog catcher, he would have to have a net and know how to catch dogs. In his pile of junk Eddie had a piece of an old tennis net. Rudy had found it some time ago, and Eddie had bought it from Rudy for ten cents—a price that seemed very high to Eddie. But now it was just the thing he needed. He found an old barrel hoop and set to work to tie the piece of net to the hoop. It took a long time, but finally it was finished. The next thing was to find a handle. He sawed a broom handle off an old broom and tried to tie it onto the hoop. Each time it fell off. Finally he went upstairs and looked in the broom closet. There he found his mother's mop and wall brush. There was a long wooden handle with a clamp on the end. This clamp fitted both the mop and the brush. Eddie felt certain that he could clamp the handle onto the hoop, if only his mother would let him borrow it.

Eddie could hear his mother walking around the second floor. He went to the foot of the stairs and called to her, "Mamma, can I borrow the handle of the floor mop?"

"What for?" asked his mother.

"I just want to try it on a net I'm making. I won't hurt it."

"All right," replied his mother, "but if you break it, you will have to buy me another one."

"Oh, I won't break it," said Eddie.

He carried the pole down to the basement, and with the help of some screws and some nuts and bolts, he finally fastened the handle to the hoop. It was a little floppy, but Eddie was quite proud of his net. Now he would go out and catch a few dogs. He guessed it would be best to begin with a little dog.

With the pole over his shoulder, the hoop swaying, and the net dangling behind him, he started for Betsy's house. After all, Thumpy, Betsy's cocker spaniel, was a little dog, and Thumpy had a nice disposition. He never snapped at anyone.

Thumpy was outside when Eddie arrived. Thumpy made some squealing sounds that meant that he was glad to see Eddie. But when Eddie raised the net high in the air, Thumpy ran under a bush and barked.

"Now, Thumpy," said Eddie, "I'm not going to hurt you. I just have to practice being a dog catcher. It won't hurt you."

Thumpy stayed right where he was under the bush. He just rolled his eyes. But he rolled them in the direction of the gate, which Eddie had left open. And Thumpy saw an Airedale coming across the street. Thumpy jumped up and shot out of the gate and joined the Airedale. Eddie ran after Thumpy with his net over his shoulder. Now he would *have* to catch Thumpy, for Thumpy was not allowed outside of the gate. As soon as Thumpy realized that Eddie was running after him, he ran faster. There was nothing Thumpy enjoyed more than a race. The Airedale, of course, ran too.

At the corner, they were joined by Chummy, the big red setter that belonged to the twins, Richard and Henry. Chummy would always join in a race. And then another and another dog joined the pack. Eddie tore along as fast as he could with his net over his shoulder. With all of these dogs, he thought, he could surely catch one.

Eddie had run around the block several times with

the dogs well ahead, when he began to feel out of breath. The net was hard to carry. It swung and pulled and was heavy. Eddie had to stop to get his breath. Almost at once, the dogs seemed to know that they were no longer being chased. They thought the fun was over. They turned around and started running towards Eddie.

Now that the dogs were running towards him, they looked like a great many more than when he was running after them. Eddie turned and started running away from the dogs. Around and around the block he went with the dog-catcher's net swinging from his shoulder, and a pack of dogs behind him. At last he ran through Betsy's gate, tripped over the curbing that edged the lawn, and fell, sprawling on the grass. The net fell on top of him, and there he was. He had caught himself in the net he had made to catch dogs.

Thumpy ran through the gate, but the rest of the dogs ran away.

Betsy, who had heard the commotion, came out of the house. There on her front lawn she found Eddie, covered with the dog-catcher's net, and Thumpy enjoying the fun of jumping all over Eddie.

"Thumpy! Come off. Stop it," cried Betsy.

Betsy finally took hold of Thumpy's collar and put him in the house. Then she went back to Eddie.

"Eddie," she said, "whatever are you doing?"

"I'm learning to be a dog catcher," said Eddie.

"Well, you caught yourself all right," said Betsy, pulling the net and the hoop off of Eddie. "And it serves you right. Why are you playing dog catcher, anyway?"

"You don't understand, Betsy," said Eddie, sitting up with the net hanging around his shoulders like a shawl. "I'm going to be elected."

"Elected what?" asked Betsy.

"Elected dog catcher," said Eddie.

"Eddie Wilson! What are you talking about?" said Betsy.

"Didn't you see the big sign downtown with my name on it?" asked Eddie. " 'Vote for Edward Wilson'? That's me."

"Eddie!" said Betsy. "It is not you. It's Mr. Edward Wilson. He's a friend of my father's, and he's coming to dinner tonight."

"He is?" said Eddie. "And you mean he's going to get elected dog catcher? Say! Maybe I could sell him this net!"

"No, Eddie," said Betsy. "Mr. Wilson isn't going to be elected dog catcher. He's going to be elected mayor."

"Well, what do you know!" said Eddie. "That man in the bus was nuts! He didn't know what he was talking about."

Eddie got up. He picked up his net and then, for

the first time, he saw what had happened. He put his hands over his face to shut out the sight. He had broken his mother's mop handle. It was cracked and almost broken in two.

"Oh, Betsy!" he groaned. "Look at Mamma's mop handle. And I haven't any money to pay for it."

Eddie picked up the strange-looking thing that was his dog-catcher's net and started for home. "So long!" he said, in a dull voice. "I think being a dog catcher is hard work."

"Good-by!" Betsy called after him.

Eddie didn't exactly hurry home. In fact, it took him a long time to get there. He walked very slowly with his bent and broken pole over his shoulder. He was not in a hurry to see his mother.

When he finally reached home, he walked around to the back of the house and sat down on the back step. He laid the wreck of the dog-catcher's net at his feet. In a few moments his mother opened the back door. She looked down at her littlest boy. His chin rested in his hands, and he looked very sad.

"Well, little boy," said his mother, "what is your trouble?"

"I broke it, Mamma," said Eddie.

"What did you break, Eddie?" asked Mrs. Wilson.

"Your mop handle," replied Eddie.

"Oh, Eddie!" exclaimed his mother. "What were you doing with it?"

"Trying to be a dog catcher," said Eddie. "I tripped."

"You know what it means, don't you, Eddie?" said his mother.

"Yes, Mamma, I know," said Eddie. "But I haven't any money."

"I guess you will have to earn some then," said Mrs. Wilson. "Better start thinking. And see if you can wash

and think at the same time. Hurry up. Dinner is almost ready."

Eddie went upstairs to get washed. He washed the palms of his hands, one ear, the end of his chin, and soaked his hair with water. In the midst of this he had an idea. He thought of the box of Wilson buttons.

He picked up the box and ran downstairs.

"Eddie!" his mother called. "Did you change your blouse?"

"I have something important to attend to," Eddie called back.

"Go right upstairs and change your blouse and come to dinner," said his mother.

Eddie went upstairs and changed his blouse.

Before he sat down at the dinner table, he placed the box of buttons under his chair. He could hardly wait until dinner was over. He thought the rest would never be ready for dessert. He waited and waited. It was awful to have to wait so long for dessert, when he had important business to do.

At last the plates were removed, and the dessert was brought on the table. Chocolate pudding! If he had known that it was only chocolate pudding, he wouldn't have waited. But having waited, he thought he might as well have a second helping. Finally his mother said that he could be excused.

Eddie slipped off of his chair, picked up his box of buttons, and said, "I'm going over to Betsy's."

"Be home by seven-thirty," said his mother.

"Okay!" said Eddie.

Eddie rang Betsy's door bell, and Betsy answered the door.

"Hello, Betsy!" said Eddie. "Did 'Vote for Edward Wilson' come?"

"Yes," said Betsy. "He's here."

"I have something I think he would like," said Eddie.

"What is it?" asked Betsy.

"Buttons," said Eddie.

"I don't think Mr. Wilson would care to see any buttons," said Betsy.

"But these buttons have his name on them," said Eddie. "They're super."

"Oh! Well, that's different," said Betsy. "Come on in."

Betsy led Eddie into the living room. There, by the

fire, sat the man Eddie had met on the bus. The man who looked like Jack Spratt. He was Mr. Wilson.

"Why, hello!" said Mr. Wilson. "If it isn't my friend who is going to be President of the United States and ride on a white horse."

Mr. Wilson held out his hand and Eddie took it.

"This is Eddie Wilson," said Betsy.

"Well, of all things!" exclaimed Mr. Wilson. "Imagine our having the same name! Now what do you think of that!"

"I have something here that I thought you would like," said Eddie, opening his wooden box. He pulled the lid off and said, "Buttons! Wilson buttons!"

"Well, upon my word!" cried Mr. Wilson. "What are you going to do with those?"

"Well, uh . . . ah," said Eddie. "Well, ah . . . I thought, maybe . . ."

"I see," said Mr. Wilson. "Well, how would fifty cents be for the lot?"

"Oh, swell!" cried Eddie. "That would be great!"

CHAPTER VIII

EDDIE THE HOOFER

EDDIE'S brothers teased him about the sign he had made, *Vote For Me*. They called out, "Hi, Eddie! Vote for me! Thought you were going to be elected, didn't you? April fool! Vote for Eddie!"

This went on so long that all anyone had to do to make Eddie's ears grow red was to call out, "Hi, Eddie! Vote for me!"

Of course, when Eddie's brothers saw that Eddie didn't like this teasing, they did it all the more, and Eddie's ears were red almost all of the time. The twins were worse than Rudy.

One morning the twins were teasing Eddie on the way to school. Joe said, "Hey, Eddie! How are the votes coming along?"

Frank said, "That's right, Eddie! Do you think you'll get elected?"

"Aw, quit it!" said Eddie.

"I saw your sign," said Joe. "*Vote for Edward Wilson*. Right across Main Street."

"Pretty swell to be mayor of the town," Frank called out.

"Scram," cried Eddie, "before I give you a poke."

At the next corner the boys met Betsy. "Hello, Betsy!" Frank called out. "Are you going to vote for Eddie?"

"Eddie's going to ride on a white horse, Betsy. 'Cause Eddie's going to be elected mayor," sang Joe.

"You mean, he wants to ride a white horse," said Frank.

"Oh, why don't you leave Eddie alone?" said Betsy. "Go pick on somebody your own size."

"Betsy always sticks up for Eddie. Betsy always sticks up for Eddie," Frank sang out in a singsong voice.

"Well, there are two of you," said Betsy. "There's only one of Eddie."

At this point, the twins ran off to join Billy Porter

and Kenny Roberts. Betsy and Eddie walked on to-gether.

"The twins make me so mad," said Eddie. "Some-times I think I'll run away."

"Oh, Eddie!" Betsy cried. "You wouldn't run away and leave your mother and father, would you? You couldn't do a thing like that."

"Well, 'course it would be very hard to leave my mother and father, but I can't live with the twins and Rudy. The twins are the worst. I sure am glad Rudy wasn't twins. But I wish I were twins, I wish, I wish."

"But think how your father and mother would feel if you ran away. They'd feel terrible. Maybe your mother would feel so terrible she would never get over it." There were almost tears in Betsy's eyes as she thought of how terrible Eddie's mother would feel if Eddie ran away.

"Do you think she would feel that bad?" said Eddie.

"Oh, she'd feel awful," said Betsy.

The children walked along in silence, while Eddie thought about this. Finally he said, "Well, maybe I'll run away anyway."

By this time Betsy and Eddie had reached the

school. "Good-by!" said Betsy as she went up the steps.

"So long!" said Eddie.

When Betsy reached the door, she turned and called out, "Eddie, you won't run away, will you?"

Eddie was running like a streak of lightning to the door of the second grade.

After school Eddie walked home alone. There were two ways to walk home, a short way and a long way. Eddie decided to take the long way.

He hadn't gone far when he met Alexander Johnson. Al was in the same grade as Betsy. Eddie thought Al was wonderful, because he could play a banjo. Al had it now, hanging from his shoulder.

"Hi yah! Eddie!" said Al.

"Hi, yourself!" replied Eddie. "Where are you going?"

"Come over here," said Al, "and I'll tell you." He motioned to Eddie to sit down beside him on a near-by doorstep.

Eddie sat down. "Eddie," said Al, "I'm goin' away."

"You mean you're moving?" said Eddie.

"Nope," said Al. "Not movin'. Just goin' away."

"But your father has a job here," said Eddie. "What's he going away for?"

"My father's not goin'," said Al. "I'm goin' by myself. I'm on my own." And Al rolled his eyes towards Eddie.

"You're going by yourself!" exclaimed Eddie. "Where are you going?"

Al waited a moment before he answered. Then he said, "To Hollywood."

"Where they make the movies?" said Eddie.

"Uh huh!" said Al. "I'm goin' to make a lot of money."

"How?" asked Eddie.

"Well, I'll tell you all about it," said Al.

Eddie put his elbows on his knees and rested his chin in his hands. His ears were wide open.

"The other day I went to the movies," said Al, "and in that movie there was a boy with a banjo, just like mine. He played the banjo, and he played it pretty good, but I think I can play better. Here's a picture of him I found in a magazine."

"Gee," exclaimed Eddie. "He looks like you!"

"Yes, he does sorta, doesn't he," said Al. "And boy! He gets a lot of money for playing that banjo. 'Course, he had a hoofer with him. And boy! That hoofer was good."

"What's a hoofer?" said Eddie.

"Why, a hoofer is a fellow that dances," said Al.

"If I just had somebody to go with me and do the hoofin', we could make money. We sure would make money!"

Eddie looked into Al's face with wide-open eyes.

" 'Course I can dance," said Al, "but it's sort of hard to dance and play the banjo at the same time.

What you need is somebody to do the hoofin' and somebody to do the playin'."

"Al," said Eddie, "do you think I could do the hoofin'?"

Al looked at Eddie. "You never danced, have you?" he said.

"No," replied Eddie. "I never tried."

"Well, you have to have loose legs to dance," said Al.

"Well, my legs are loose," said Eddie. "Look!" Eddie stood up and shook his leg. "It's awful loose," he said.

Al got up. He began to strum on his banjo and tap one foot. "Now you just do what I do, Eddie," he said.

Eddie began to tap one foot.

"Now, let it slide a little bit," said Al, as he began to tap with both feet.

Eddie tried tapping with both feet.

"That's pretty good," said Al. "Keep your legs loose. Just like rubber."

Eddie tried to make believe his legs were rubber.

"Let your arms dangle," Al called out. "Just like rubber."

Eddie let his arms dangle. He was doing pretty well now. Keeping time to Al's banjo wasn't hard for Eddie because he had played the triangle in the kindergarten orchestra when he was only five years old. He had learned then about rhythm.

Finally, when Al stopped playing, Eddie took a rest. "Do you think I'm good enough?" he asked.

"You're not bad," said Al. "And you'll get better along the way."

"Are we goin' today?" asked Eddie.

"We sure are!" said Al. "We gotta get started."

"Isn't it miles and miles?" said Eddie.

"Sure is!" said Al.

"Are we going to walk?" asked Eddie.

"Well, not exactly," said Al. "I figured we could play and dance on the street, and 'course people will give us money, and then we can use the money to get to the next town."

"Oh, that's a good idea," said Eddie.

" 'Course, we'll have to eat," said Al.

"Oh, sure," said Eddie.

"I figured we could roast potatoes," said Al.

"Oh, yes!" said Eddie. "I like roasted potatoes."

"Maybe we should roast a couple before we start," said Al. "Have you any money?"

"No!" replied Eddie. But to make certain, he looked through all of his pockets. "No. Not a cent," he said, when he had finished.

"How are we going to get potatoes if we haven't any money?" asked Al.

"Don't know," said Eddie, "but we have to get potatoes."

"Sure do," said Al, shaking his head. "Can't start out without a couple of baked potatoes."

"Maybe we could sell something," said Eddie, emptying his pockets.

While Eddie looked through his collection of bolts, nuts, screws, nails, tin foil, bottle caps, broken chalks and crayons, bits of string and marbles, Al emptied his pockets. Between them they found nothing that they felt they could sell. They put everything back in their pockets and walked across the street to a grocery store. There they stood, looking at large sacks of potatoes piled on the sidewalk.

"What do you boys want?" asked the grocer.

"We want a couple of potatoes," said Eddie.

"Where's your money?" asked the man.

"We haven't any," said Eddie.

"Do you think I give my potatoes away?" asked the man. "Here, if you boys want a couple of potatoes, carry these sacks around to the back of the store. Pile them on the pavement in the back street against the wall of the building. And be sure not to put them on the elevator. Then I'll give you each a potato."

"Okay!" said Eddie, taking hold of a sack of potatoes.

Eddie pulled at the sack but he couldn't lift it. "It's heavy, isn't it?" he said to Al.

"Sure is," said Al, "but we can do it together."

"Careful you don't break those sacks," said the owner. "They're only paper, you know."

The boys carried sack after sack of potatoes from the front pavement to the back street. There they put them in a neat pile against the back wall of the store. Just as they placed the last sack on the top of the pile, they heard a bell ring. It seemed to come from under the potatoes.

"What's that?" said Al.

"I don't know," said Eddie.

The bell kept ringing and the boys kept staring at the pile of potatoes. Then the sacks started to move. Right before their eyes, the pavement under the potatoes seemed to be moving. It was coming up in a peak. It was upsetting the sacks of potatoes. It was throwing them to right and to left. The sacks were breaking, and potatoes were rolling all over the pavement and out into the street.

The grocer came running out of the back of his store.

"You dummies!" he cried. "You put the potatoes on top of the elevator door. Didn't I tell you not to put them on the elevator? Now look at my potatoes! All over the pavement! All over the street!"

"I didn't know that elevators came up through pavements," said Eddie.

It took Eddie and Al a long time to pick up all of the potatoes. They had to put the loose ones in baskets. The sacks that had not broken they piled by the back door, not on the doors of the elevator. Finally they were through, and the grocer gave them each a potato. "You can have more if you want," said the man.

Eddie and Al had handled so many potatoes they

didn't care to have more than one apiece. However, by the time they found a place to build a fire, and had made it out of a wooden box, they had forgotten how hard they had worked over the potatoes.

When the fire had burned long enough to make bright embers, they put their potatoes in. The boys sat beside the fire, watching the potatoes and talking about the money they were going to make. Finally the red embers turned to ashes, and they had to poke around with sticks to find their potatoes. At last they rolled them out, looking pretty black.

"I guess they're awful hot," said Eddie.

"They have to cool," said Al.

While they waited for them to cool, the sun began to go down.

"Now, we'll have to do some playin' and dancin'," said Al. "We gotta earn some money for bus fare. We have to get out of this town tonight, sure."

"That's right!" said Eddie. "It's a long way to Hollywood. We have to get started. Are we going to sleep on the bus?"

"Of course we're going to sleep on the bus," said Al, picking up the two potatoes.

He handed one to Eddie and the other he put in his pocket. "Come on," he said. "Let's start the show."

"Where are we going to do it?" asked Eddie.

"We'll go over to one of the streets off Chestnut Avenue. There we'll get the men getting off the bus. If we do it on Chestnut Avenue, we'll get chased, 'cause it's crowded."

Eddie and Al hurried along until they reached the street that Al thought was best. Then Al began to strum on his banjo. "Now, get goin', Eddie. Get goin'," said Al.

"But there isn't anybody watching me," said Eddie.

"That doesn't make any difference," said Al. "You just get goin' and they'll come and watch."

Eddie began to tap to the music. Al kept saying over and over, "Loosen up those legs. Loosen up those arms. Shake 'em. Shake 'em."

Eddie was so busy learning to dance, and Al was so busy teaching him, that neither of the boys noticed that a tall man had stopped to watch them. It was dark now, and the man stood in the shadow of a tree.

Al zing-zanged on his banjo, calling out, "Shake those legs. Shake 'em! Shake 'em!"

Beads of perspiration stood out on Eddie's forehead and upper lip as he went on and on with the dance.

At last Al stopped playing, so Eddie stopped dancing.

"Am I a good enough hoofer?" said Eddie.

Then the man stepped out of the shadow of the tree. To Eddie's great surprise, he handed him a nickel. Eddie looked up, and he looked up into his own father's face.

"Not bad, son," said his father, as he handed a nickel to Al, too.

Eddie was so surprised he stood like a marble statue, holding the nickel between his thumb and forefinger.

"Come along now," said his father. "You should have been home long ago. It's almost dinner time. Come along with me. We don't want to keep Mother waiting."

"But, Papa!" Eddie began. "I . . . you see . . . Al and I . . ."

"Come, Eddie," said his father. "It's getting late."

"Well, you see . . ." said Eddie.

"Eddie, I haven't time to waste," said his father. "Mother asked me to stop and get ice cream for dinner.

Today is the twins' birthday. She made a cake."

"She did!" cried Eddie. "Jeepers!"

Eddie placed his hand in his father's and said, "So long, Al! Be seein' you!"

"So long!" said Al. "Sorry you're not goin' along."

Just at this moment Al's father appeared. "Hello, Al!" he said. "Time for you to be coming along home. Mommy's cooking fried chicken tonight. Fried chicken and apple pie."

"Fried chicken!" said Al, falling into step with his father. "I sure do like fried chicken. And apple pie, did you say?"

"Apple pie," said his father.

"My!" said Al. "Nothin' better in the world than Mommy's fried chicken and apple pie."

"What was that you just threw in the gutter, son?" said Al's father.

"Oh, that was just an old roasted potato," said Al. "It was sorta burnt."

That night when Eddie's mother went upstairs to say good night to little Eddie, she found him almost asleep. In one black hand was clutched what looked like a large black stone.

When his mother leaned over him, he held out his hand and murmured, "Mamma, here's a roasted potato for you. I cooked it."

His mother took the potato and kissed him. Then she said, "Thank you, darling. Shall I keep it for you?"

"No," replied Eddie. "It's sorta burnt."

CHAPTER IX

WHERE WAS AL?

THE following morning when Eddie woke up he thought of Al. He wondered where Al was now. He guessed he was on a bus somewhere. He was sorry he wouldn't see Al again, but he was glad he hadn't gone with him. Mamma and Papa had given the twins bicycles for their birthday, and the twins had said he could ride on them. The bicycles were a little big, and Eddie's legs were a bit short, but he could manage to reach the pedals. "The twins are certainly super!" thought Eddie. "They are certainly super! Just imagine! Two brand new bicycles in the garage! Boy! If I had gone with Al, I never could have ridden on those bicycles."

At breakfast Eddie said, "Did you know that Al Johnson's gone to Hollywood? He's going in the movies."

"What's he going to do in the movies?" asked Rudy.

"He's going to play his banjo," Eddie replied.

"I don't believe it," said Joe.

"It's the truth," said Eddie. "He told me all about it yesterday. He started for Hollywood last night."

"Oh, go on! I'll bet he'll be in school today," said Frank. "He's not good enough to get in the movies."

"Yes, he is," said Eddie. "Al's super. He's going to make a lot of money."

"He was just kidding you," said Rudy. "I'll bet he'll be in school this morning."

On the way to school Eddie met Betsy.

"Oh, Betsy!" cried Eddie. "You should see the bicycles the twins got for their birthday. They're beauts! All red and black. And I can ride on them. The twins said I could. Boy! It's swell to have twins, 'cause you get two of everything. You just ought to see those two bicycles in our garage. They are sure super-duper!"

"Then you're not going to run away?" said Betsy.

"Oh, no!" replied Eddie. "I didn't mean it when I said I was going to run away. But say! Did you know that Al Johnson is going to be in the movies?"

"What do you mean?" asked Betsy.

"Why, he's gone to Hollywood," said Eddie. "He's going to play the banjo in the movies, and make a lot of money."

"How do you know?" asked Betsy.

"I saw him yesterday and he told me," said Eddie. "He went on a bus last night."

"He did!" exclaimed Betsy. "Isn't that wonderful!" Betsy thought that being in the movies was the most exciting thing that anyone could do.

When she reached school, she went into her classroom. She was in the fifth grade now. Her teacher was Miss Williamson. Betsy looked across the room to the place where Al always sat. The place was empty.

Betsy turned to Ellen, who sat behind her, and said, "Did you know that Al Johnson has gone into the movies? You know how wonderful Al is when he plays the banjo. Well, he's gone to Hollywood, and he's going to be in the movies. Isn't that marvelous!"

"He is!" said Ellen. "Oh! Isn't that wonderful!"

"What's wonderful?" asked Billy.

"Al Johnson's gone to Hollywood. He's going to be in the movies," said Ellen.

"Who said so?" asked Billy.

"Betsy heard it this morning," said Ellen.

"What's Al going to do in the movies?" asked Billy.

"You know how good he is playing the banjo," said Betsy. "Well, he's going to do it in the movies."

"How did he get in?" asked Christopher, who had joined the three children.

"I don't know," said Betsy. "Maybe one of those men that they send all over the country heard him play."

"Oh! You mean a talent scout," said Billy. "Gee! Maybe he was right here in this school the last time Al played with the orchestra."

"I wish he had seen me," said Betty Jane. "I'm going to be a movie star when I grow up. My mother says I'm much prettier than Peggie O'Mallie, and that I can act better. And my dancing school teacher says if a talent scout saw me, he would put me in the movies right away. My! I wish I had danced the day the talent scout was here and heard Al play."

"I guess Al will get a thousand dollars a week," said Kenny Roberts, who had joined the group.

"Boy! That's money!" said Billy.

"My aunt was in Hollywood last year," said Betty Jane, "and she saw the houses that the movie stars live in, with swimming pools and everything. I guess Al will have a beautiful house with a swimming pool."

Just then the bell rang, and the crowd of children around Betsy broke up. They all sat down at their desks.

Miss Williamson, who had been writing sentences on the blackboard, went to her desk.

"Good morning, boys and girls," she said.

"Good morning, Miss Williamson," the class replied.

"Let us repeat the Twenty-third Psalm," said Miss Williamson. The children began, "The Lord is my Shepherd," and said it through to the end—"I will dwell in the house of the Lord forever."

Then Miss Williamson called the roll. When she reached Al Johnson, she said, "I wonder where Al is this morning."

This was just what the class was waiting for. Nearly every hand flew up.

"Well!" said Miss Williamson, in surprise.

Betty Jane was so anxious to tell Miss Williamson

the news about Al that she looked as though she would shake her hand off.

"Betty Jane," said Miss Williamson, "do you know where Al is?"

Betty Jane got up with a swish of her skirt. "Oh, yes, Miss Williamson," she said. "Al moved to Hollywood. He's going to be in the movies. A talent scout was here in this very school, and he heard Al play the banjo with the orchestra, and now he's going to put Al in the movies."

"This is very surprising!" said Miss Williamson. "Are you sure it's true?"

"Oh, yes, Miss Williamson," said Betsy. "Al told Eddie Wilson yesterday. He said good-by to Eddie yesterday."

"It's very strange," said Miss Williamson. "He didn't speak to me about it."

Al's seat remained empty day after day. The second week, a large poster was placed outside of the neighborhood movie house. Above the poster were the words, "COMING ATTRACTION." On the poster in large black letters was the name of the picture, "BANJO BLUES." It showed a man in a full dress suit. He was wearing white gloves and he had a high hat in his hand. His mouth was wide open for he was singing. Behind him stood a little boy playing a banjo. Another one was dancing.

The children saw it on their way home from school, and in no time at all a crowd had gathered. Almost all of the fifth grade were there, as well as little Eddie, the twins, and Rudy.

"There's Al!" Eddie cried. "There he is, playing the banjo. I wonder who the hoofer is with him?"

"What's a hoofer?" asked Billy.

"Don't you know what a hoofer is?" said Eddie.

"No. What is it?" said Billy.

"Why, a hoofer is somebody that dances," said Eddie. "Al wanted me to go with him and be the hoofer."

"That's the craziest thing I ever heard you say," said Rudy. "You know that isn't true."

"It is so, true," said Eddie. "Al showed me how to do it." And with this, Eddie began to tap dance the way Al had taught him.

The children formed a circle around Eddie and watched him.

"You're not good enough to go in the movies," said Betty Jane.

"Al said I was good enough to go with him," said Eddie.

"Well then, why didn't you go?" asked Betty Jane.

For a moment Eddie couldn't remember why he hadn't gone. Then he said, " 'Cause it was the twins' birthday."

"Eddie!" cried Betty Jane. "That's the craziest reason I ever heard. I just wish Al had asked me."

The children could hardly wait until the Saturday of the following week. They were all going to the show to see Al.

When Saturday afternoon arrived, there was a long line of children at the ticket window, long before the window was opened. All of the fifth grade were there, as well as Eddie, the twins, and Rudy. Over the entrance in huge letters were the words, "BANJO BLUES with Joe Alison and Peggie O'Mallie."

The children were a little disappointed not to find Al Johnson's name on the sign, but they were going to see him in the picture. They were very much excited and chattered like magpies.

At last the ticket window was opened, and one by one they bought their tickets. A boy at the door took the tickets from them, and they went inside. Immediately there was a rush for the front seats, and a great deal of noise. Some of the children changed their seats four and five times. They were so afraid they wouldn't have a good seat from which to see Al. There were voices: "No, you can't sit there! I'm saving that seat." "No fair saving seats!" "Hey! That's my seat. Scram!" "Hi! Bill!" "Hi! Don!"

Betty Jane had brought a bag of jelly beans. In the rush for the front seats, she knocked the bag against the back of one of the seats, and the bag broke. Jelly beans rattled all over the floor and rolled in every direction. They sounded like beads.

For fifteen minutes the children waited for the show to begin. They chattered, they whistled, they clapped their hands. They didn't like waiting.

At two o'clock the lights went out and the picture began. It was a gay picture with lots of singing and dancing. The children enjoyed this, but all eyes were watching for Al. Finally, on a street corner, lighted only by the moon, the small boy with the banjo appeared. The little tap-dancing boy began to dance.

"There he is!" cried Eddie. "There he is!" His voice was drowned out by the clapping. The children clapped and clapped. Some even stamped their feet.

The children were sorry that this part of the picture was so short and that, in the moonlight, they couldn't see Al very clearly. But perhaps in the next picture Al would have a bigger part.

It was too bad there was only one show on Saturday afternoon. All of the children would have stayed to see it over again. But when the lights went on they had to leave. There was a great rush to get out, just as there had been a great rush to get in. The fifth grade came out almost in a solid bunch. "Did you see Al?" they asked each other. "Wasn't Al good?"

"Gee! Al was wonderful, wasn't he?" said Eddie, as he joined the group.

The whole crowd pushed out of the front doors onto the sidewalk. There, looking up at the poster showing the banjo player, was a boy. It was Al Johnson. He turned away and saw the crowd of children. His face lighted up with a broad grin. "He's good, isn't he?" said Al, pointing to the banjo player. "I nearly missed it. I just got into the movie in time to see him."

For a moment the children stood speechless. Then Betsy found her voice and said, "Al! Wasn't that you?"

"Didn't you go to Hollywood?" cried Eddie.

"No," replied Al, "I never did get started."

"Well, where have you been all that time?" cried Billy.

"Oh," said Al, "I had the mumps."

CHAPTER X

ANY OLD JUNK TODAY?

NEVER a week went by without Eddie bringing home some piece of what Eddie called "valuable property," and his father called "junk."

The family always knew when Eddie had brought home a new treasure. Eddie would always announce at dinner, "I had a very enjoyable day today." When Eddie said this, his father would look at his mother and say, "Uh! Oh!"

After dinner his father would go down to the basement, and there he would find another piece of junk added to Eddie's collection.

"Now, see here, Edward!" said his father one evening. "This junk collecting has reached the limit. What happens every week? I'll tell you. On Friday night every man in this neighborhood puts his rubbish out for the rubbish collectors, and every Saturday a large part of it lands in our basement. Now, I am tired of it. The basement looks like a junk shop, or worse. It looks like a dump. This thing has got to stop."

Eddie looked very downcast as he said, "You were glad when I brought home the telegraph pole, weren't you?"

"Well, that was different," said his father. "Moreover, that is past. I'm talking about the present. This junk collecting has reached the limit. We will never get all of this stuff out of the basement."

"But, Papa!" said Eddie. "I don't want it out. It's my valuable property."

"Valuable property!" exclaimed his father. "Junk! Nothing you ever bring home is worth the room it takes."

"I brought the telegraph pole," murmured Eddie.

"Well, yes, the telegraph pole," said his father.

The following Saturday Rudy and the twins went

on a hike with some of the boys in Rudy's class in school. Eddie wanted to go, too, but they said that he was too little. He felt very badly until his mother said that he could go for a drive in the car with herself and his father. They were going out into the country to see if they could find a shop where they could buy a nice tilt-top table.

It was a beautiful day, and as they drove along the roads Eddie saw the cows and the horses on the farms. He saw men working in the fields. He read the signs along the road. *Fresh Eggs. Broilers.*

The first time Eddie saw the word "broiler," he said, "What is a broiler?"

"It's a young chicken that is small enough to broil," said his mother.

Eddie could read most of the billboards. He found it exciting to be able to read, to have letters mean something.

They had been driving for about an hour when Mr. Wilson brought the car to a stop in front of a store. There was a large sign hanging outside which Eddie could not read. "What does that sign say, Pop?" asked Eddie.

"It says *Antiques*," said his father.

"Are we going to see Aunt Teek?" asked Eddie. "Does she own the store?"

"Not Aunt Teek," said his father. "Antiques. Antique means old. When you see that sign, it means that the shop sells old things."

"You mean junk?" said Eddie. "Sounds exciting!"

"No, indeed!" said his father. "These things are valuable."

By this time, Mr. and Mrs. Wilson and Eddie had gotten out of the car. They walked up the path to the porch.

"I never saw a store with a porch before," said Eddie.

"Well, you're in the country now," said his mother. "They often have porches."

Eddie looked around the porch. It was full of all kinds of objects. Among them were some huge kettles, some fire screens, and brass and iron andirons. There were long iron forks and tongs for handling the logs in a fireplace. There was an old wooden bench, and a big wooden box with pictures painted on it.

"Gee!" said Eddie. "It sure looks like junk."

The windows of the shop were filled with shelves, and the shelves were covered with glass vases, cups, plates, saltcellars, pitchers, and sugar bowls.

The inside of the store was crammed with furniture —tables, chairs, chests of drawers, and cabinets full of china. The store was big. It seemed to Eddie to go back, and back, and back.

"Jeepers!" thought Eddie. "I'll bet a fellow could find some very valuable property around here."

While his father and mother were busy talking to the owner of the shop, Eddie wandered toward the back of the place. He looked over the shelves; he peered into open boxes and barrels. Finally he went through a doorway into what seemed to be a store-room. There he came upon a man opening a barrel.

"Hello, son!" said the man. "Can I do something for you?"

"I'm just looking around," said Eddie. "My father and mother are out there." Eddie pointed to the front of the store.

In a moment Eddie's eyes fell upon something that interested him very much indeed. On a shelf stood an old carriage lamp. It was rusty and covered with dust.

"Do you want to sell that lamp?" Eddie asked the man who was opening the barrel.

The man looked up. "I guess we do," he replied.

"How much is it?" asked Eddie.

"Oh, 'bout a quarter," said the man.

Eddie reached into his pocket and pulled out all of his money. He had seventy-five cents. Twenty-five cents was his weekly allowance. His father had given it to him that morning. The other fifty cents he had earned during the week, delivering orders for Mr. Henderson. His regular boy was away.

"Okay!" said Eddie. "I'll take it."

The man took the lamp from the shelf and blew the dust off of it. "Want it wrapped up?" he asked.

Just then Eddie's eye fell upon another interesting object. It had been hidden behind the carriage lamp. "What is that?" asked Eddie, pointing to what looked like a small iron urn with a wheel on each side. It, too, was rusty.

"Oh, that?" asked the man, lifting it down. "That's an old-fashioned coffee grinder."

"Those wheels are super!" said Eddie, his eyes very big. "How much is that?"

"Oh, I guess I can let you have that for fifty cents," said the man.

Eddie looked at the coffee grinder for a few moments. Then he said, "I'll take that, too."

"Want them wrapped?" asked the man.

"Yes, please," replied Eddie, taking a look out to the front of the store. His mother and father were busy looking at some dishes.

"Suppose I put them in this carton," said the man.

"That will be fine," said Eddie.

Eddie watched the man put the coffee grinder into the bottom of the carton. Then he put the lamp on top. When he folded over the flaps, they didn't close because the end of the lamp was too long. The man tied a piece of cord over the top to hold the flaps down, but the end of the lamp still showed. "I guess that will do," he said.

"Oh, sure!" replied Eddie, as he handed over his seventy-five cents. "That will do."

Eddie decided to go out of the back door with his package. Once outside, he ran to the car. He thought it would be best to put the package in the trunk of the car. His father had left the keys in the car, so Eddie unlocked the trunk and placed the package on the shelf. Then he locked the trunk and put the keys in his pocket.

Eddie sauntered back to the front porch. He was examining a broken lock when his father and mother came out.

"Look, Papa," said Eddie. "This is a swell lock."

"It's a piece of junk," said Mr. Wilson. "No more junk is going into our house, Eddie. Put it down."

Eddie put the lock down and walked to the car with his father and mother. "You left the keys in the car, Pop," said Eddie, handing over the bunch of keys.

"Oh, thanks, Eddie," said his father.

They all climbed into the car. Eddie sat between his father and mother.

"Didn't they have any table, Mother?" asked Eddie.

"No, dear," replied Mrs. Wilson. "But they expect one in next week."

For some time they drove in silence. Then suddenly Eddie said, "Well, I had a very enjoyable time."

Mr. and Mrs. Wilson immediately looked down at Eddie. He looked up at them with a sweet smile on his face. Then they looked at each other. Mr. Wilson put on the brakes and stopped the car. He turned around and looked on the back seat of the car and on the floor. There was nothing there.

"What did you say, Eddie?" his father asked.

Eddie looked up and said, "I just said I've had a very enjoyable time."

Mr. Wilson took the keys from the car, opened the door, and stepped out. He walked around to the back of the car, opened the trunk, and there was Eddie's package.

Eddie, standing beside his father, said, "Please, Papa, it isn't junk. It's swell stuff."

"Eddie!" said his father, "when I said, 'No more junk,' I meant it. This isn't going another foot of the way home." To Eddie's amazement, his father placed the package in a ditch beside the road.

As Mr. Wilson leaned over, he saw the end of the carriage lamp sticking out of the top of the carton. He pulled off the cord, and lifted the lamp out of the carton.

"Say!" he cried. "Why, this is a carriage lamp. Say! This is mine. Why, I have been wanting one of these for a long time. I want it to go on the post at the front gate. Why, this is a beautiful carriage lamp. It just needs to be refinished. Well, now! This is mine!"

"But I bought it, Papa," said Eddie. "I paid for it."

"Well, I'll give you a dollar for it, Eddie," said his father. "How is that?"

"Okay!" said Eddie.

In the midst of this discovery, Mrs. Wilson joined Eddie and his father.

"Look, Mother!" Mr. Wilson cried. "Look at this fine carriage lamp. This is mine."

Mrs. Wilson was busy looking into the carton which still lay in the ditch. "Why, look at this old coffee grinder!" she cried. "Oh! What a duckie coffee grinder! Oh, this is mine! These old coffee grinders make the most beautiful lamps you ever saw! Mrs. Porter has one, and it's lovely. With a coat of red paint, this will be perfect."

Mrs. Wilson held the old coffee grinder very lovingly. "Oh! This is mine!" she said.

"But I bought it, Mamma," said Eddie. "I paid for it."

"Oh, well. I'll give you a dollar for it," said his mother. "Is a dollar all right?"

"Ah, Mamma!" said Eddie. "I like that coffee grinder. I like it a lot."

"Well, I'll give you two dollars for it," said his mother. "That's a lot of money, Eddie. Think how rich you will be."

"Okay!" said Eddie.

The three went back to the car. Mr. Wilson went first, carrying his carriage lamp. Then Mrs. Wilson, carrying her coffee grinder. Little Eddie brought up the rear, with three dollars in his small fist.

When they were almost home, Mr. Wilson said, "By the way, Eddie, how much did you pay for that lamp?"

"A quarter," said Eddie.

"And how much did you pay for the coffee grinder?" asked his father.

"Fifty cents," Eddie replied.

"Not bad!" said his father, looking at his mother.

"You know, Papa!" said Eddie. "I've been thinking. Do you know what I'm going to be when I grow up?"

"No," replied Mr. Wilson. "What are you going to be?"

"I'm going to be a junk man," said Eddie. "That's a good way to get rich."

"How about letting me go into business with you?" asked his father.

"Okay, Papa!" said Eddie. "Will we have a store?"

"Oh, certainly!" said his father. "And we'll have a big sign that says, *Wilson and Son—All Kinds of Junk.*"